James W. Thompson

# An Inaugural Sermon preached at Jamaica Plain

Anatiposi

James W. Thompson

# An Inaugural Sermon preached at Jamaica Plain

Reprint of the original, first published in 1859.

1st Edition 2023  |  ISBN: 978-3-38230-956-5

Anatiposi Verlag is an imprint of Outlook Verlagsgesellschaft mbH.

Verlag (Publisher): Outlook Verlag GmbH, Zeilweg 44, 60439 Frankfurt, Deutschland
Vertretungsberechtigt (Authorized to represent): E. Roepke, Zeilweg 44, 60439 Frankfurt, Deutschland
Druck (Print): Books on Demand GmbH, In de Tarpen 42, 22848 Norderstedt, Deutschland

# The Great Commission:

AN

# INAUGURAL SERMON

PREACHED AT

## JAMAICA PLAIN (WEST ROXBURY),

APRIL 24, 1859.

---

## BY JAMES W. THOMPSON.

---

Published by Request.

BOSTON:
CROSBY, NICHOLS, AND COMPANY,
117, WASHINGTON STREET.
1859.

# SERMON.

---

Matt. x. 7, 8: " AND, AS YE GO, PREACH, SAYING, THE KINGDOM OF HEAVEN IS
AT HAND. HEAL THE SICK, CLEANSE THE LEPERS, RAISE THE DEAD, CAST
OUT DEVILS: FREELY YE HAVE RECEIVED, FREELY GIVE."

WHEN these words had passed from the lips of the
Son of man, the New Dispensation, of which he was
the Mediator, was fairly inaugurated. Till then, it had
existed only in prophecy, in vision, in the thoughts of
devout men who waited for the consolation of Israel,
and in those rudimentary preparations by which the
Twelve had been educated for receiving their august
commission, and for doing the superhuman work it
imposed. Now it becomes a fact, palpable, to be
known and read of all men; central and centralizing
to the thought, imagination and genius, the philo-
sophy and literature, the faith and aspiration, of
the whole human world; potent with self-evolving
powers, which no demands can ever exhaust, and no
opposition effectually resist; destined also to universal
recognition, and a sway without limit in space or
time. No longer is it a sublime conception alone in
the mind of Christ, an abstract, formless, inoperative

force in his bosom; no longer a stupendous plan struggling to actualize itself, but waiting opportunity. Its hour is come, the fulness of the time; and now it shall stand forth a majestic reality, a church, a kingdom, and the amazing achievement it contemplates be at once commenced.

Regarded in the issues it involved, this was the grandest moment in human history; which, indeed, was not a moment, but an age, and series of ages, spreading out indefinitely, covering all time, extending into eternity, and peopling the heavens with earth-cradled saints. Could the Twelve have foreseen the consequences with which it was fraught; had they even apprehended, with any approach to its full extent, the personal responsibilities it would cast upon them, and the career of peril and hardship it was opening before them, — they would have shrunk from the undertaking, appalled by its fearful magnitude and endless relations.

So it is always. Every man holds in his bosom possibilities yet to be made actual, which, if they could be laid before him in one view, would utterly overwhelm and confound him. The futurity of our own being is, therefore, wisely concealed from us. No prophecy discloses it. Dark shadows are hung over it, hiding even from imagination the developments of which the germs lie hid within, and which are to become personal history. Could any one, — the youth, for instance, just emerging into manhood; the teacher, with his young charge around him; the man of business, his head teeming with enterprises; the rich man, with golden opportunities of usefulness; the maiden at her bridal hour, in the flush of beauty, and amidst the tears and rejoicings which lend a chastened brilliancy to the dear but solemn rite; the minister of religion, entering the sphere of his appointed service, and assuming his holy trusts and cares with immortal beings so wonderfully organized, so variously endowed, in capacities so unequal, in sensibilities, affections, cravings, aims, so unlike, for the field he is to tend and till, — could these take in at a glance all the issues involved in their several positions, the view would paralyze them; they would shrink from the responsibilities; they would be incapacitated for pursuing the good bound up for them in the vast and various combination of results. It is no denial of a privilege, then, but a gracious ordination of Heaven, that we must walk by faith, not by sight; that the soul's path is illuminated, not by the dazzling effulgence of an all-comprehending knowledge, but by the mild stars of promise and hope. Count it not misfortune, but rather advantage, that to-morrow is hid; and what it may bring forth, shrouded in mist. In calm trust, wait the revelation.

All history is a series of surprises, the rudiments of which, as also their order of evolution, were laid in the bosom of the first man when God breathed into him a living soul. Higher, grander, more wonderful they become as the ages roll on, displaying more and more His wisdom who planned them. Observe their sublime unfoldings with grateful reverence, but seek not to know them before the time. Secret things belong to God only, and are to be disclosed, not when man's curiosity asks, but when His pleasure determines. The ignorance of the Twelve, when they stood before their Lord to receive their high commission, was their content and safety; not to know or to be able to forecast the future, their wisdom and strength.

I have said, and repeat, that the date of the apostles' commission was the sublimest moment in human history. Whether viewed in the contrasts it exhibits, — so much power blended with so much weakness, — the Son of God intrusting to twelve rude, unlettered men of a benighted province, speaking the poor dialect of a language scarcely known abroad, a work so stupendous; or whether contemplated in the results to be wrought out, — the overthrow of hoary idolatries and proud philosophies, which boasted as their founders the highest names known amongst men; the enthroning of a new Man, of obscure origin, a Galilean, as sovereign in the realm of spiritual truth, before whose imperial sway Grecian culture should bow its garlanded head, and Roman bravery lay down its invincible arms; the erection of a world-wide empire, that should at length swallow up every other, and itself, permeated in every part by the spirit of truth and love, be transfigured into a church universal, without spot or blemish, — whether beheld in either of these points of view, nothing sublimer can be imagined as transpiring on earth than the act of Jesus in sending forth his apostles.

But the commission they received did not die with them. It is of abiding force, renewed from generation to generation; keeping alive a perpetual apostleship to repeat the same glad tidings, and to perform the same ministries of mercy. To-day we hear the voice which the Twelve heard, saying, "Go, and proclaim, The kingdom of heaven is at hand. Heal the sick, cleanse the lepers, raise the dead, cast out devils: freely ye have received, freely give."

Listening reverently to the voice, and earnestly desiring to obey it, let us now search into the meaning of the message to be announced, and into the nature of the work to be done.

I. The message.
II. The work.


I. "The kingdom of heaven is at hand." It would be a strange thing to-day for such a band of men, starting together, to travel through the length and breadth of the land, making only this proclamation.

Doubtless there was a certain strangeness, even then, in their appearance and words. But whatever of singularity there might have been was in a measure relieved by a general preparation of the mind of the age. When they went forth in Galilee, Judea, Samaria, and announced that the long-deferred hope of Israel was at length accomplished, that the great redemption foretold from the beginning had begun to fulfil itself, the people's heart everywhere was ready to respond, "Amen! Blessed is he that cometh in the name of the Lord!" Expectation, kept alive and transmitted from generation to generation, in each, as it succeeded, becoming more intense, was then brightening to its culmination; and this prepared the people for the messenger who should proclaim that the time of desire was accomplished, the day of fulfilment at hand. But not what they expected appeared; and so deep and bitter disappointment, or scornful disbelief and derision, was the first effect, when it began to be seen that the new kingdom was no earthly monarchy; its throne, no visible seat of majesty and power; that its laws were broader than any civil polity, higher than science had traversed, or art symbolized, or the loftiest forms of poetic speech more than faintly illustrated. Their visions of deliverance, of State grandeur, of overflowing treasuries and irresistible arms, — the ideal glory of all human kingdoms, — were to be realized indeed, but in a way they never dreamed of.

Only as symbols were they true. Material splendor and magnificence could only represent, and that but dimly, the true kingdom of heaven, which cometh not with observation; which embraces the world of thought, desire, emotion, affection, aspiration; which has the conscience for its throne, the heart for its palace, the eternal God for its sovereign, and, for its conquests and trophies, the vices that destroy the body, and the passions that war against the soul. It is a kingdom founded in everlasting truths, and sustained by principles of order, beauty, and rectitude, which have their root in the Infinite Mind. But its truths and principles are not subtle and incomprehensible abstractions: they are all combined, expressed, and represented in the life and character of a single PERSON, and that Person no other than the Son of God. Thus the new kingdom is, in substance, a new theocracy, — God reigning over men, and in the midst of them; the regency being vested in his beloved Son. It is, in other words, Christianity taken up into a living man born of the Highest, in his bosom enthroned, in his life illustrated, by his death and resurrection completed, sealed, established, as supreme law and an ever-abiding spiritual force over man and in man, to govern him, to renew him, to inspire him, day by day, till he becomes perfect as his Father in heaven is perfect. It is the Word, not in the silence in which it was "in the beginning" with

God, but spoken and speaking; "the Word made flesh, and dwelling amongst us," radiant with holy beauty, its heart beating and its countenance flushed with divine love and mercy; the Word going forth from lips touched with living coals from heaven, to kindle, in its progress, soul after soul into a quenchless zeal for truth and righteousness, till the holy fire-baptism has cleansed and saved the world. Wherever the truths and principles of Christianity are acknowledged; wherever the God and Father of our Lord Jesus Christ is believed in so as to be felt, loved, worshipped; in whatever soul the Eternal One is consciously enshrined, according to that high axiom of St. John, " He that dwelleth in love dwelleth in God, and God in him," — there the kingdom of heaven has come; there the benign and eternal reign of wisdom and love has commenced; there religion is fulfilling its office; there peace and joy in the Holy Ghost are the soul's abiding possession.

It cannot be too strongly felt — what the Twelve were instructed to proclaim — that the kingdom of heaven is come, is here. We have not to look abroad for it, to cross perilous seas, to visit strange lands, to inquire of the masters of learning, or to follow the guidance of new stars, in order to find its capital and court; but to seek it here, amongst ourselves and within ourselves.

There are those who are ever looking backward

for their kingdom of heaven. Their golden age is far behind, — in buried glories, in perished institutions, in virtues that once flourished, in an innocence and peace no more to be repeated. Their light is the lamp of memory. Cities, empires, arts, literatures, that have passed away, are their study and delight. They live in the past. There are others, again, whose kingdom of heaven is in the distant future. Their imagination is for ever busy in portraying the scenes and circumstances of an age yet to dawn, or a world yet to come, which they paint in hues of a brilliancy to which nothing in the present, however enchanting, is worthy to be compared. This is a great mistake; it is to forget the message, " The kingdom of heaven is *at hand.*" God did not exhaust his goodness in the earlier ages, nor has he reserved all its outpourings for a future day. No: he has surrounded the present with heavenly attractions; crowned to-day with imperial glories; festooned the passing moments with flowers fresh-plucked from paradise; brightened the immediate scene with rays effulgent as those which fell upon the world when the morning stars sang their first hymn, and all the sons of God shouted for joy. The kingdom of heaven is come in the plenitude of its grace and truth. The two great commandments are its fundamental law. The incomparable Sermon on the Mount, the profound spiritual inductions of St. John, the unsurpassed argumentations and melting heart-utterances of the great apostle to the Gentiles, reveal its spirit and purpose. It is come, and still coming. More and more, its mighty energies are diffusing themselves. Deeper and deeper, its great life is searching the secret windings of the human heart. Farther and wider spread the rays of its unclouded Sun over the waste places of error and the dismal vales of sin. Yes, the new kingdom is come. Its benignant sway is felt as an instant reality. To every community of believers the saying is true, " The kingdom of heaven is within you," — within *you*. According to the measure of their faith, the King is seen by them in his beauty and royal apparel; his voice heard in its awful authority; his life perceived as impersonated truth, virtue, sanctity, hope, eternal and complete. And by them, in the uprightness of their daily walk ; in the pureness of their hearts, or the sighings of their penitence; in the overflowings of their mutual charity, and the holy fellowship of their worship; in the steadfastness of their zeal for the enlargement of the borders of Zion, and the displacement of whatever exalts itself against the will of God, — each day and hour, in high places and in obscurest corners; in the private ear of trembling penitence and solitary struggle, and on the house-tops of stolid security and luxurious re-pose; to the young, undisciplined to saintly patience and prayer ; to the middle-aged, imprisoned in the outward and sensuous, but striving to be set free; to the old, imploring God to be their stay and staff, that they may depart in peace, — the announcement is to be made, by look and speech and rapturous song, and that silent eloquence of the Spirit's grace which is more convincing than voice and words, "The kingdom of heaven is at hand." Such, then, is the message.

II. And, now, what is the WORK? "Heal the sick, cleanse the lepers, raise the dead, cast out devils: freely ye have received, freely give." No miraculous power rests on us as on the apostles, and we can use only such gifts as we receive. Yet the Lord is with his faithful servants still, to aid them in every ministration of their hearts and hands to the relief of human suffering and woe, and the cure of those maladies of which sin is both cause and consequence. Their work at this day, though not in all respects identical with that of the primitive heralds of the gospel, is not essentially different. It is a service of man in the name of Christ, and its characteristic feature is its *humanity*. It illustrates that saying of an apostle, that pure religion is manifested in visiting the widow and fatherless in their affliction, and in an unspotted life. It is not, like the priesthood of every other religion, mainly an altar-service or a ritual performance, a special work of the temple and the holy day; but it is a daily and continual offering at the sweet shrine of kindness and mercy,— a life from which blessed influences spring with no sabbath-pauses, rising as fragrant incense over man's misery, and penetrating, as a celestial aroma, the polluted air of the world. It takes its Lord for its model. As he went about healing the sicknesses, soothing the sorrows, pitying the injuries, lifting the burthens, of men; so his servants follow him, humbly seeking to make their presence a blessing and a joy to those unto whom they are sent: and, as there was no form of misery which did not command his sympathy, so there is none which they can willingly overlook. As against every inveterate wrong under which men groaned, however intrenched and defended by custom, policy, or power, he lifted up his voice in stern and terrible rebuke; so they turn the weapons of their warfare upon all the crimes and oppressions that fill the earth, or any portion of it, with wailing and tears, and that hinder the triumphant march of truth and righteousness to their destined glory. Evil, the *root* of evil, — *that* is to be destroyed. The wretchedness of man or woman — *that* is to be commiserated. The tears that stream from the eyes of penitence, or that soil the cheeks of bereavement,— *they* are to be wiped with hands of tender condolence. The demons which sin conjures up into the maddened brain — *they* are to be rebuked and cast out by the spirit of holiness and love. The dead in trespasses and sins — *they* are to be roused by the trumpet-call of the gospel, and, if possible, warmed into life in the bosom of Christian sympathies and affections. Religion, as they administer it, is the friend and helper of man. It multiplies the loaves of the poor. It offers willing shoulders to the burthens of the weary and careworn. It puts sight into the touch of the blind, and speech into the fingers of the mute. To the houseless, it gives a home; to the cripple, a hospital; to the wayward and intractable youth, a School of Reform; and to the frail penitent, a Refuge from temptation and the scorn of the unfeeling. It watches with the sick, by star and by sun, as an angel of peace; and it points the faith of the dying to the eternal mercy-seat, and the heaven which surrounds it. Nor is this all. Authority to heal and restore, to bind up and console, carries with it the duty of protecting against evil. So it seeks to purify and elevate the fountains of social influence; to clarify the springs of moral life; to make the home, the school, the state, nurseries of virtue and spiritual strength; and especially to fence round the young, just beginning the immortal race, with safeguards — in their tastes, affections, fears, and hopes — against the approaches of temptation, and the fearful ruin it so often succeeds in effecting.

Ah, how sadly has the moral and humane part of

Christianity been neglected hitherto! Had the gospel been exhibited by its servants, during the eighteen
centuries of its life, in the spirit of its author; had
it been made to appear more the present friend and
benefactor of man, and less the dogmatic combatant
or bigoted devotee; had the world seen it more in
the acts of a genial messenger of deep and genuine
philanthropy, penetrating the darkest scenes of human
trial with a word to cheer and a hand to bless, and
less in splendid and pompous ceremonies, obscure
and unbelievable creeds, and solemn pietisms; had
it borne on all its banners waving over its commerce
and trade, proudly floating from its domes of legisla-
tion and justice, unfurled in new and strange fields
by its own soldiers, that one word which syllables
the dearest name of God, and of which itself is the
highest expression, — the poor, the outcast, the en-
slaved, the suffering, everywhere and from every cause,
would not only have been vastly reduced in numbers,
but those who still remained would have been in
warm and living sympathy with it, and so in a condition to receive the fulness of its life and light. Oh!
when shall the lesson taught by the ministry of Jesus
be understood, — that to protect the innocent, to guide
the young, to reclaim the wanderer, to lift up the
fallen, to cheer the desponding, to encourage the penitent, to bind up the broken-hearted, to strive manfully
against evil, and to labor diligently for good, — that

this work of *humanity* is the allotted task of each disciple according to his ability, and the only evidence that will be admitted, in the Great Day, of his fitness to be a companion of that twice-born brotherhood of whom Christ is head?

Such, then, is the message, and such the work, of the Christian ministry. With this message and work it has fallen to me, in the providence of God, to be charged. I come to you to-day, my friends, bearing the message, " The kingdom of God is come nigh unto you," and charged in my conscience and soul, by Him whose servant I am, to give unto you freely that which I also have received, for your redemption from sin, and edification in righteousness ; for your security amid the perils of prosperity, and your solace under the pains of adversity ; for the solution of your doubts, and the confirmation of your faith ; for the guidance of your souls to the rest of consummated virtue and saintly holiness in the bosom of the Father of mercies. Standing here, for the first time, in this special relation to you, it may well be supposed that some curiosity is felt in respect to the views which may govern the administration of my office. But this curiosity, if it exists, can be gratified only by statements the most general. Young ministers are accustomed, on occasions like this, to exhibit a programme of what may be expected of them, and what they expect of their people ; but it is a programme which is seldom followed on either side. In the fervors of a hitherto unbaffled zeal, they often pledge themselves to herculean labors, forgetting that it is only sons of Hercules who are equal to them. I offer to you nothing of the kind. I cannot tell what I shall preach, and what I shall do; save that, as grace is given to me, I will declare, and labor to extend, the kingdom of heaven, present amongst men in the historical Christ and his word, and in all hearts in which the gospel has entered as a subjective reality; and will seek to give full effect here to all those truths, sympathies, and charities which lighten the weight of pain, disappointment, sorrow, and sin, and which tend to lift young and old, the strong and the weak, the fresh and the weary, into the serene gladness of true religion. I would seek to make doctrine practical; the highest truth, a life within: for, if left in the form of ideas in the mind, truth is only like the raindrop upon the leaf. It may glisten in the sun, and add a moment's brilliancy to the object; but it is of no service to the tree. But, when ideas are translated into principles and deeds, they are like the raindrops, penetrating to the roots, and sending new energy and vital sap into every branch. I am here as a minister of the New Testament, — the dispensation of grace and truth by Jesus Christ. I am here, not as one called by you simply, but sent by my Master, — both mine and yours. Am I asked to indicate the basis

of my teaching? My answer is in the words of
Paul to the church of Corinth: " Other foundation
can no man lay than that is laid, which is Jesus
Christ." No new-fangled gospel of to-day or yesterday
or to-morrow; but that which is the same yesterday,
to-day, and for ever, — unchanging truth, immortal
goodness, everlasting life, the supreme authority and
dominion of Him who is over all, and through all, and
in us all. Taking my place within the new kingdom,
with my people around me, I move forward with it
in its aggressions upon the domains of the world,
opposing whatever would obstruct its march, and
giving my whole heart to whatever commends itself
to my judgment as calculated to further its beneficent
ends. Details are unnecessary; but this must be said,
this you would all wish me to say, that, *as I hear, so
shall I speak ;* trying to keep my ear open to every
whisper of the Spirit's voice, and my tongue clear to
make report thereof to you. Not taking counsel
of man, except for the sake of his help to the under-
standing of the word of Christ and the law of God;
not weakly yielding to the suggestions of fear or of a
short-sighted expediency, nor defiantly challenging
censure and opposition; not hesitating to espouse an
unpopular cause when it bears the marks of right
and truth, nor disdaining that which is popular from
a paltry pride of singularity, or contempt of public
opinion,— freely and fearlessly, in the love of man and

STOP.

---

the love of God, I pray that grace may be given me to declare the whole truth as it is in Jesus, and that you may have the same grace to profit withal.

There has been much controversy about the freedom of the pulpit. I have but little to say on that point. The pulpit *is* free; and no honest man wishes it to be otherwise. By its very nature, it is free. The moment it is restrained of its liberty, it ceases to be a pulpit, and becomes a piece of fancy-work in wood, with a speaking automaton behind it. The imputation of a desire to interfere with its freedom would be felt, by every honorable mind, as an insult. But it is useless, and, worse, it is harmful folly, for it to be for ever vaunting its freedom and provoking assaults. Let its action, rather than its boastful lips, declare its independence; and let it use its freedom with discretion, lest it become a snare and a hinderance to the truth. It is a sad mistake of the pulpit, when it assumes that its hearers are at odds with it on vital points, and are to be worried and goaded into agreement. Its function is not to drive, but to win, souls into the fold of the Great Shepherd, —

> "By winning words to conquer willing hearts,
> And make persuasion do the work of fear."

All here, in these calm moments of meditation, and in this vestibule of the heavenly temple, are not merely willing, but in their souls *demand*, that the truth should be preached freely, fully, earnestly, and without reservation. Every ingenuous mind would be ashamed of the minister of religion who should keep back any part of his message from imbecile compliance with prejudices, opinions, or caprices, reported to exist around him. Every true man would cry, "Let him be anathema!" He is false to his trust; and, being so, is false to his people.

But every part of his message, let him remember, is to be delivered as from the Lord, and not from himself, in the very spirit of his heavenly Teacher, calmly and without passion; avoiding all harsh and irritating tones and terms; in the deepest reverence for truth, and with that strong conviction of duty which would prompt him to say, "Woe is me if I preach not the gospel!" Never let him throw down the gauntlet to any of his parishioners, and brace himself in the attitude of a pugilist. Let him assume that they are all his friends; as they are ostensibly, by the fact of their assembling for worship in the name of Christ, *his* friends, and subjects of his divine kingdom. Contests between pastor and flock are fatal to all religious life and growth. If the latter succumb, they feel that a galling priestly autocracy is established over them; if the former, he feels that the word of God is thenceforth bound in his person, and can no more utter itself except in broken sentences and pusillanimous tones. Let all such strifes be avoided, as leading, by a swift and sure decadence, to destruction.

The church — by which I mean the congregation assembling for worship — is an organic whole, made up of members differing in original endowments, in culture, in moral traits, in pursuits, in the measure of their interest in the great questions which society and religion agitate, and in many other things; yet all associated for common objects, and all equally entitled to every privilege belonging to the organization. The incumbent of the pulpit is, under Christ, the head of this body; standing, by consent of all, to each and every member of it, without distinction, in one and the same relation; knowing no rich, no poor, no party, no clique; a common centre of religious influence, a common instructor, guide, and friend. The church is one body; the ministry, not a separate estate, but a constituent membership. This idea excludes all hostile antagonisms, and is the true basis of a living harmony and a hopeful progress. The primitive apostolic church, guided by the inspired master-builders who laid its foundations, rested its strength in its unity. Uniformity of belief, thought, character, it did not demand, but unity of spirit and aim, — unity in the broad purposes for which it was gathered, and unity in the sense of brotherly fellowship. It was a household sacred to love and mutual edification, in which the forbearance, patience, charity, generosity, of the gospel were to be freely exercised; in which each was to feel himself in a manner protected by all; in which the weak were to find succor in the strong; the easy victims of temptation, pity from the upright and secure; those who saw the truth but dimly kept where its beams fell, by those who were more fully enlightened. If one were overtaken in a fault, he was to be — not exscinded, not held up to scorn, not branded with the scarlet letter, but restored in the spirit of Christian meekness and compassion. When it is assumed that each member of a church is a separate power in it, — the minister with the rest, — and those subtile, undefinable, but most potent relations, which, in its normal state, constitute its organic unity, are lost sight of; when one member, cleric or laic, feels that the church is his to bind and loose, to make and unmake, to *control*, instead of regarding himself as belonging to it, as part and parcel of its vitality and working force, as bound up with it for a common end, and obliged to view its welfare as his own personally, — confusion and every evil work ensue.

This must suffice. I have spoken to you of the greatness of the commission of the ministers of the word, of the meaning of their message, of the nature of their work, and have indicated a general view of the manner in which it may be expected that the ministry will be exercised here. To say that I look for your friendly co-operation would be needless. The affectionate smiles of the young, the efficient good-will and support of the middle-aged, the genial companionship of them whose day of active labor begins to put on sunset hues, — for these I look with entire confidence. To feel that they would be withheld, would be the signal for me to retire at the close of this service. Equally unnecessary would it be to attempt to point out *your* duties in detail: you know them already. You will not expect from this connection large immediate results. I come a sower, bearing seeds of the kingdom of heaven, — they are called seeds of righteousness, peace, and joy in the Holy Ghost, — to sow as one blind; not knowing whether in stony places or on good ground, but committing the whole field to the nurture of Heaven's sun and rain. This seed is of slow growth: spiritual harvests are not ripened in a day or a year. Let us pray, that, in the *end of the world*, — your world and mine, — the angel reapers may find some sheaves here fit to be gathered into the Father's garner. Let us take encouragement from the old promise, " He that goeth forth and weepeth, bearing precious seed, shall doubtless come again rejoicing, bringing his sheaves with him." The day itself is auspicious, — the day which saw Him rise, in whom the world is risen into a new hope, and rising still into a new life, — the day which gave to man victory over the grave, and made him fellow-heir with angels to the infinite treasures of God. Let us borrow from it all hopeful and cheering auguries, and go forward to the duties of our sacred relation, and continue in them, as under the light and joyful inspiration of Easter morning. " For this cause I bow my knees unto the Father of our Lord Jesus Christ, — of whom the whole family in heaven and earth is named, — that he would grant you, according to the riches of his glory, to be strengthened with might by his Spirit in the inner man ; that Christ may dwell in your hearts by faith ; that ye, being rooted and grounded in love, may be able to comprehend with all saints what is the breadth and length and depth and height ; and to know the love of Christ, which passeth knowledge, that ye might be filled with all the fulness of God.

" Now unto Him that is able to do exceeding abundantly above all that we ask or think, according to the power that worketh in us, — unto Him be glory in the church by Christ Jesus, throughout all ages, world without end. Amen."

A

# Valedictory Discourse

DELIVERED IN

## THE FIRST CHURCH, BEVERLY,

JULY 4, 1858.

---

By CHRISTOPHER T. THAYER.

---

Published by Request.

---

BOSTON:
CROSBY, NICHOLS, AND COMPANY,
117, WASHINGTON STREET.
1858.

# DISCOURSE.

---

WHEN, my friends, some months since, I was led by the providence of God, and by duty to others and myself, to decide on resigning the pastoral office I had long sustained among you, a tide of emotion came over me such as I had never before experienced, and could, only under like circumstances, be realized. How could it be otherwise, in view of dissolving the holy relation that had subsisted between us for much the largest part of my life, and of the lives of most of you, — longer than no small portion of our number have lived; with all its duties and pleasures; its toils and cares and trials; its tender friendships and delights of sacred confidence; its sweet communions in the temple, at the table of remembrance, in the social circle, within the domestic retreat, in the chamber of sickness, the house of mourning and death; all the scenes, joyous or sorrowful, of weal or woe, of the soul's discipline, through which we have together been led? Prominent among the emotions thus excited was gratitude that our mutual esteem and affection were unabated, but rather strengthened, or at least more sensibly felt, at thought of the dissolution of our connection as pastor and people; and that I might leave you strong in yourselves; strong, I trust, also in the Lord; and prosperous, — prospering most in the things belonging to your higher welfare. Above all was the sense of accountability for the discharge of the unspeakably important trust committed to me, in which were involved the rise or fall, the great and lasting good, the very salvation it might be, of many; and God only knows the sincerity and fervor of the supplication which it prompted, and which rose from this bosom, for his merciful forgiveness of any unfaithfulness of mine to that trust. Then there was regret, not unlike that which the sensitive spirit often feels for friends gone from earth or about departing, that I had not contributed more to the improvement and happiness of those from whom, as their appointed spiritual teacher and friend, I was soon to be separated.

Instead, however, of yielding to vain regrets, I resolved and endeavored to redeem the time; to make my last days in your service my best; to render departure, if possible, more fruitful than permanence; and so, in my humble measure, to resemble those who, by their deaths, have done more than by their lives. And I rejoice to bear testimony, that, in this effort, you have cordially, efficiently, nobly co-operated. The period that has intervened has for me, in truth, been occupied with "crowded life." Years have seemed compressed into months; these into weeks; and so with minuter divisions of time. Time, nevertheless, waiting for none, has kept on in its course; and now the shadow on the dial, the hand on the hour, as a guide-post on the way in the journey of life, indicates unerringly that the point of divergence has been reached, and that the parting words must be spoken. It only remains, therefore, for us to gather up, and give fit utterance to, the recollections, lessons, purposes, feelings, and hopes appropriate to the occasion.

In so doing, I will adopt for my text, and as corresponding to the first and chief topic on which I shall speak, the language of the Apostle Paul in his First Epistle to the Corinthians (xv. 1 and 2): "Moreover, brethren, I declare unto you the gospel which I preached unto you, which also ye have received, and wherein ye stand; by which also ye are saved, if ye keep in memory what I preached unto you, unless ye have believed in vain." So would I, in humble imitation of the apostolic chief, recall to your memory what for many years I have preached to you; which you have so candidly received; in which, I trust, you are firmly established; and which, if not unduly presuming, I would hope may so far accord with the gospel of Christ, which is the power of God unto salvation, as — by being kept in living remembrance, and believed, not in vain, but practically and with the heart — to issue in the saving of our souls. It cannot be otherwise than well for us, before we part, to attend thus to a main branch of my ministerial office, — to its objects, the mode of its discharge, and especially to the views I have aimed to present and inculcate.

Preaching is a most important part of the Christian minister's duty. The command, "Preach the word," — given to the earliest, and intended to apply to all succeeding, teachers of Christianity, — he will, if rightly inclined, labor earnestly to obey. He will spare no exertions he can properly make to prepare himself for the faithful performance of this essential function. For this will he be much in prayer, in meditation, in study, in fervent and persevering exercise of his intellectual and moral faculties. For this, also, there must be system. Without system of some sort, no science or art — certainly not the science of divine truth, and the art of living a holy life — can be well taught or well learned. Christian preaching, in short, to be best executed, and accomplish its legitimate ends, must be thoroughly systematic. Not that this trait, wherever existing, will be invariably manifest and recognized. When pulpit instruction proceeds on a fixed, well-defined, comprehensive plan in the preacher's mind, that plan may still not always be obvious to the hearer, who may be unable, while following out its details, to keep steadily in view its outlines. The fluctuating nature of our congregations tends peculiarly to prevent many from comprehending and remembering it. From various causes, the aspect of religious assemblies is constantly changing; the presence of those composing them being, for reasons sufficient or insufficient, in large proportion, irregular and uncertain. Owing to the number from among us engaged in seafaring life and pursuits abroad, our own congregation is subject to more than common fluctuation of attendance. Thus, and in various other ways readily suggesting themselves, are most of the members prevented from forming a connected view of the system of preaching, if such there be, pursued by him who stately fills the sacred desk. For its comprehension, it therefore becomes necessary occasionally (and than this no time could be more suitable) to direct our eye back on the whole track gone over; to observe the lights that have illumined and guided our progress; to review the general principles on which we have proceeded; to group, as it were in one, the different views that have been taken. We may thus have in our mind's eye a map of the region traversed; just as the traveller ascends the topmost peak or dome, that he may take in at a glance the varied features of the landscape through which he has passed. By so doing, he obtains more exact and vivid impressions of the whole scene; discerns its lights and shades, its beauties and defects; learns the bearings, distances, and magnitudes of the principal objects; ascertains in what respects his way might be improved; and fixes in his memory landmarks for his direction hereafter. So may we receive juster ideas of the nature and relative importance of the truths and rules to which we have been accustomed to listen together; be assisted to correct the errors taught or imbibed; and as seekers of heavenly knowledge, and pilgrims to the celestial land, the better to shape our future course, by an impartial, full survey of the system of religious teaching that has with us been pursued.

The plan of preaching I have adopted, and endeavored to carry out, has been based on the belief, that Christianity is at once a profound science to be acquired, and an immense field of duty to be explored and cultivated. Religion is as much a science as any subject for man's investigation can be. It has its appropriate provinces for inquiry, its general principles and laws, its peculiar sources of truth and evidence. All these it has been my aim to discover, and to draw from in such degrees as should best subserve the grand purposes for which preaching was divinely instituted.

Taking the Bible as the rule of faith and practice, I have sought to show it worthy to be so received by proofs from within and without itself, — such as the credibility, interest, and value of its contents; their revelations of surpassing sublimity, beauty, joy, hope, awe, of wisdom relating to this world and the one to come; their practical design and admirable adaptation to its furtherance; their consistency with the operations of Providence and with human experience; their conformity to the teachings of nature and reason; and the support they derive from credible historical testimony, especially from their own history and influence, ever since they were given to men. The truths, which on careful inquiry I have obtained from them, have, as seemed fitting and requisite, been presented to you, together with the grounds on which they rest. Their precepts have been laid before you, as circumstances appeared to demand, in what I conceived their length and breadth, and application to the whole duty of man. The examples they set forth of the great and good, and of the low and bad, have been held up as models or warnings for our conduct. The illustrations which the historical parts of Scripture receive from and impart to cotemporaneous common history, have, as opportunity offered, been remarked. Characters and events, whether pertaining to individuals or communities, have been drawn from other quarters besides the sacred records, and employed for instruction, admonition, and encouragement, and thus made to give light and enforcement to abstract truths and rules. Events particularly, occurring within the sphere of our own experience, and appealing directly to our own hearts, have from time to time been noticed; and I have felt that such events, prosperous or adverse, or however affecting us, if duly improved by the preacher, might be eloquent and effective preachers of righteousness, — be indeed ministering spirits sent from above to sanctify and save. In truth, wherever in any of the departments of nature; in any of the sciences and arts; in any of the manners and customs, laws and institutions, prevailing or that have prevailed; in any of the beings or things throughout the material or spiritual universe, — lessons of religious wisdom might be gathered, and motives for obedience to them gained, there I have not hesitated to be a reaper and gleaner, that what was thus procured might contribute to the edification of my hearers. I have, moreover, aimed to bear constantly in mind, that all discoveries of truth are valuable mainly as they are applicable, and actually applied, to promote moral and religious growth in the soul.

Here I would say, that increased observation has tended to confirm me in the impression of the absolute boundlessness of the sources whence the Christian preacher may draw for the purpose of illustrating, impressing, and giving practical effect to, religious truth. Time would fail me now for merely enumerating them, as it would for presentation of the different lights in which it has, according to my ability, been brought before you. Instead of attempting to survey the wide space thus indicated, I will briefly review the principal topics of my preaching; on which I have chiefly enlarged and insisted, because I believed them consistent with the letter, expressive of the spirit, and eminently promotive of the true ends, of the gospel. They range themselves naturally in two classes.

First, There are those common to most, if not all, Christians. Included in them are the perfect God; an all-sufficient Saviour; the immortal soul of man; its spiritual capacities and aspirations; its exposure to temptation, error, and sin; the Divine Spirit working in it; Christ's mission and agency in enlightening, converting, redeeming it, and bearing it on to a heavenly destiny; faith of the reason and with the heart; repentance; progressive holiness; looking to Scripture for inspired guidance; the commandments and ordinances, and walking in them blameless;

2

righteous retribution; all the duties implied in holy living, or in preparation for peaceful death. On these and like themes have I mostly dwelt, and delighted to dwell, in my public ministrations. They involve the sum and substance of our religion; they are momentous in themselves and their consequences; they are inexhaustible in their supplies of wisdom, solace, strength, joy. Even when partially obscured and imperfectly apprehended, they are not without a gracious and restoring influence. A virtue goes out from them to the humble seeker, with vision dimmed and feeling after it, as there did to the believing woman, who only touched the hem of the Master's garment. They open a fountain, into which the very spirit of healing has descended, where every moral malady may be removed. Tables are spread by them in the wilderness of earth, at which they who hunger for righteousness may be filled. By them are we joined in full communion with all that love the Lord Jesus in sincerity, and are brought into large, loving, blissful fellowship with —

"The holy church throughout the world."

Under this head, let me specify another topic; namely, philanthropic enterprise. Feeling, with many of you, deep interest in this marked feature of our age, and recognizing its claim to the attentive consideration of every religious society, I have not overlooked it in my preaching. Could the great causes of peace, temperance, freedom; the thousand charities that are abroad; and, above all, the diffusion throughout the world of the religion from which so largely they spring and are fed, — could these fail to be advocated by any really Christian pulpit? You, if I mistake not, will testify, that, in advocating them, I have avoided trench-

ing on others' rights; that, while I have exercised my own,
— among them, that of free suffrage, — I have not availed
myself of the pulpit as a vantage-ground from which to
descend amid the dust of political and worldly contests, or
to invade unjustifiably another's province. Still, I have
rejoiced to bear a part, humble though it might be, as a
preacher as well as a man, in the great conflict going on
with social evil; from this elevated stand-point — beholding
the wrongs by which society, and at least persons, classes,
races in it, are darkened and oppressed — to proclaim, in its
remedial and beneficent efficacy, the golden rule of right
and love; firmly and openly to avow my own, and be the
official exponent of your, active and warm interest in fur-
thering those vast objects of reform and benevolence, toward which the mighty philanthropic heart of Christendom
is yearning with a depth and fulness and power that will
become more full and deep and powerful, till they shall be
secured. And I have felt, that so I was discharging a high
duty of my office, and helping to bring us into sympathy
with the body of genuine believers, — into harmony with
the essential unity of spirit in the Christian church.

That church, nevertheless, has its divisions and sub-
divisions. Hence arises the other class I referred to,
of subjects for pulpit discussion. This class includes
points of sectarian belief and action. They result naturally from differences in mental constitution, in circumstances and influences operating in earlier or later years, in
the modes of investigation pursued, in the varying methods
and aspects in which scriptural truth comes to the mind;
not to mention other sources whence they rise. Happy we,
who accept them on the cheerful and broad ground of their
not being bars to Christian communion, or fatal to the soul's

peace and safety. Yet many of them are important in themselves and their bearings, and are not to be ignored by any enlightened pulpit. As such I regard those by which, as Unitarians, we are distinguished. Among them are the strict unity of God; the identity of the Spirit of God with his person and influence; Christ's inferiority to his and our Father, and his absolute dependence on him; human nature created pure, and depraved by conscious, actual sin alone; regeneration needed by men in precise proportion to their having thus sinned, and to be obtained just as they endeavor to attain it; divine aid — not fitful like the wind, nor more mysterious than that — ever ready and sure to attend with favoring breezes the spread sail and onward course in the work of spiritual reform and progress; a future state of rewards and punishments, corresponding exactly to the virtues and vices of this; moral discipline and opportunity for restoration not being banished thence, and no soul whom the all-loving Parent created, and whose destiny he foresaw, being doomed to hopeless and remediless misery. Mere faith, too, — faith even in the mercy of God, or any thing the Saviour has done or suffered; all substitutes, real or fancied, for personal righteousness; all sacrifices, except that of a contrite and devout heart, of living conformity to truth and right, — are, under the administration of the universal Father, ineffectual toward securing his approval, and the greatest good which man may acquire.

These sentiments I early imbibed, and may indeed be said to have inherited; my own father, and his before him, having in substance held and preached them. On that as well as other accounts, I was led to exercise stricter caution, in fact jealousy of association and prejudice, in investigating their grounds and tendencies. The more I have inquired, observed, experienced of them, the more have I been convinced of their soundness and value. I have, and have long had, an unwavering conviction, that they accord with the tenor of Scripture, and will bear the test of its most searching criticism ; that they are of the essence of the primitive Christian belief. I hold them to be chief elements in the stream of pure religion flowing down from the apostolic age, which — as the fabled river of Greece, that, losing itself in the earth, flowed on through the sea, and mingled its waters with those of a distant land — has, often and for long periods, been overlaid by false and vain philosophies, dark and chilling dogmas, waves of superstition and fanaticism, but has emerged at length, without having parted with any of its original properties, in its purifying and life-giving efficacy ; its advancing current having, on either side, banks smiling with moral verdure, bloom, and fertility ; vines wide-spread, and laden with rich clusters of knowledge and virtue ; stately trees of spiritual life, whose branches reach far, and bend with immortal fruit.

In plain terms, I believe that the distinctive faith we embrace has, from the first, been working, and working mightily, to further the advance of civilization and Christianity ; to extend the dominion, and secure the ultimate triumph, of truth, charity, and righteousness in the world ; to modify and rationalize, so to speak, — that is, render consistent with reason as well as Scripture, — the opinions, and elevate, refine, and liberalize the practice, of other sects besides our own ; to rebuke and check bigots and fanatics ; to resist and eradicate the vices and crimes by which souls are degraded and ruined, by which the face of society is marred, and the root of bitterness planted and made to flourish in its otherwise pleasant garden. I believe also, as

I have confidence in human progress, that our peculiar faith is destined to be a main instrument of that progress. Not the half of its power has been told, far less put forth. Some of the finest spirits among men have been nurtured under it, and many more shall be touched by it to yet finer issues. Rightly understood and applied, it is adequate to regenerate the world; to rid the Church of the corruptions that through ages of darkness have settled upon her, stained her beautiful garments, and eaten into their very texture, and to bring her back to primeval simplicity and purity; to convert and revive the soul, wherever and whenever needing to be converted or revived; to quicken and invigorate it for all Heaven-appointed labor and conflict, and conduct it to a height of knowledge, a depth of peace, a variety, beauty, glory, of virtue, hardly yet conceived by the mind of man.

With such convictions of the nature and tendency of our faith, I have delighted all along, in private and in public, to cherish and maintain it. On my coming here, this was distinctly announced as a specific object of exertion. Accordingly, the first organization established in the parish, after my settlement, was a society auxiliary to that excellent institution, the American Unitarian Association, to which liberal contributions have annually been made, and from which has been received much more than an equivalent in the diffusion of correct religious sentiments. That Association I would, in passing, commend to your continued interest and aid. By preaching, especially, have I aimed to explain and inculcate our denominational doctrines. Impressed fully with their truth, their worth, their being the brightest manifestation yet made to man of the wisdom and saving power of God, I have proclaimed them from this desk in no faltering tone, no ambiguous phrase, no mystical garb; with no threading of dubious mazes of speculation, in which they or their spirit might be lost; with nought to extenuate, unless it be our want of fidelity to the precious faith we are privileged to hold, and cannot hold too dear; with no leaning or turning or shifting to the right hand or the left, to one side or another, or many sides; no attempt at compromise in things not admitting of it; at reconciling differences in their nature irreconcilable; in fine, with plainness and directness belonging to and altogether becoming our peculiar principles, when set forth by themselves, or placed in contrast, as might be required, with those from which they differ. When, however, 1 have deemed it needful to comment on these last, and point, by way of caution, to their nature and effects, it has been sought to be done with mingled frankness, candor, and charity; with the conviction entire that no diversity of opinions can fatally affect salvation; that to fear God and work righteousness are the sole conditions of acceptance with him; that the well of water Jesus has opened, springing up to everlasting life, is neither Samaritan nor Jewish, nor exclusive of any sincerely thirsting who will draw and drink of it.

It has been my endeavor to fulfil the preacher's duty in a spirit, at once catholic and eclectic, of liberality and goodwill, and receptive of good whencesoever offered. I have welcomed, and doubted not my hearers would welcome, any truth, from whatever source obtained, that tended to promote enlightened and practical religion. No pulpit, I conceive, has been more substantially free than this, for the period we are reviewing. It has never been closed against the utterance of what was honestly and deliberately believed to be truth. A prevailing rule, notwithstanding, has been, that the truth should be here spoken in love. The last

thing, or one of the last, to be tolerated among us, is violent
denunciation of others differing in sentiment from ourselves.
Ministrations from widely different quarters, and varying
materially from our theological standard, have, you will
remember, often been cordially received by us. It is but
just to you and me, on this occasion, to say, that if there be
not the fellowship, including ministerial exchanges, to be desired between ourselves and other denominations around us,
it is not for want of a willingness to that effect on our part,
distinctly expressed and well understood. With the views,
which I know you equally with me delight to cherish, of
enlarged Christian intercourse, I could not for a moment
consent that any part of the odium which properly attaches
itself to the division-walls by which Christians are separated
and set in hostile array, or any portion of responsibility for
the tremendous evils thence resulting, should rest here.
Let us hope, and let us do what we can to realize the expectation, that this occasion of offence, this weapon by
which Religion is wounded in the house of her friends, —
even their unnatural and unhallowed estrangement, — shall
one day, and ere long, be for ever removed ; when there
shall no more be repulsion, but attraction, between the
Christian spheres, — attraction holy and irresistible, because
it shall be seen and acknowledged, as of the primitive
disciples, "how these Christians love one another."

Though dwelling thus much on preaching, I am not un-
mindful of the not less important service of worship. Of
this, the sacred song is a part of no little consequence, —
more than is generally apprehended; and we may con-
gratulate ourselves that here it has been conducted so
uniformly with a taste, fervor, and solemnity fitted to make
melody in the heart to the Lord. But prayer, — the joint,

highest offering of the worshippers, the ascent of the mind
to God, communion in spirit with the Father of spirits, —
prayer, undoubtedly, is foremost in the services of the sanctuary. Words fail to express my sense of the solemn
responsibility he is under who is commissioned to lead in it.
Even when conducted after established forms, it must, to be
justly effective, be bathed in his spirit, and receive new life
from his engagedness and piety. When — as seems to me
better, more impressive, more availing — he unites studious
preparation to spontaneity in its performance, he must draw
from the deep springs of his own best thoughts and emotions ; must call on his soul and all within it, that he may
pray, and bring others to pray, aright, — sincerely, fer-
vently, with due regard to events and circumstances,
necessities and sins, to every relation and duty. Bowing,
a creature of earth, before the Majesty of heaven and earth,
and feeling that, therefore, his words should be few, — rather
that he would be dumb, his lips sealed in silence, — he is yet
expected to give utterance to the feelings and wants of his
fellow-worshippers. Deeply conscious of imperfection and
error ; abashed, covered with confusion, and blushing with
shame ; ready to hide his face in the dust at the felt presence
of the all-pure One, — he yet must stand forth to make confession for the sins of the people, and supplicate for others
the forgiveness he deems almost too much ·to ask for himself. Profoundly sensible of his own weakness, and need of
strength from above ; bending, it may be, with the weight
of trial and infirmity, — he is expected to cheer the droop-
ing spirits, to lift up the hands, strengthen the hearts, and
address to the only sufficient Helper the desires, of the
congregation. Dim though his own taper may be, it must
suffice to light and keep alive a flame of devotion in many

souls. With these views and feelings have I led in your devotions. Pure joy would there be to me in believing, that, by any effort of mine, they had been kindled, raised, and sanctified ; too great the happiness of at last finding it associated with the higher services of them who have gone from us to join in the worship of the heavenly temple, and now tune to that their golden harps.

All the ministrations of this house I have aimed so to perform as to have them answer to the true nature and ends of public worship. What is its nature ? What are its ends ? It is a means of bringing man near to his Maker and near to his fellow-man ; of causing heart to meet heart, while the soul meets her God. It draws men, by the cords of love, and joint, faithful service, to their common Father. It is a cement, by which to unite all, of whatever age, capacity, or condition, in an indestructible union. By bringing them before the universal Former and Disposer, it makes all earthly distinctions vanish, and the essential equality of souls to be manifest. While it requires and nourishes self-respect, it requires also and nurtures mutual respect between brethren and men. They whom it assembles, that together they may meditate, inquire, listen to the word read and preached, sing and pray, will be likely to be inclined thereby to regard the more both themselves and one another. A firm foundation is thus laid for stability, order, and prosperity, alike in individuals and in society. It affords also a blessed refuge from the storms of life, sweet solace to the sorrowing and tried, and, by the horns of the altar, a stronghold and a way of escape to the tempted and sinful. It has solemn relation to the life that now is ; its observance or neglect often corresponding to rise or fall in worldly condition. Unspeakably more does it concern the life to come; making the house of God the gate of heaven. No wonder, then, that many of the wisest and best should deem it their high duty and privilege to sustain public worship by their personal presence and liberal aid. Especially may the minister of religion be expected to direct to this object a large portion of his energies. To invest it with most attractiveness; to produce just appreciation of its nature and purposes; to assist in promoting its true ends, that have just been indicated, and are expressed by the single phrase, pure and practical Christianity, — all this it has been my endeavor to keep steadily in sight, and, as far as might be, effect by the solemnities of social worship. This, with the increasing demand for knowledge, and for variety and novelty in its presentation, has been, and must still more be, no slight task. If, in the course of my ministry, the charm of novelty may have been wanting; if things old as well as new have been produced, — I would have you consider the occasion for repeating old truths, line upon line, precept on precept, that exists in the intellectual and moral condition of the world and of every congregation. And I would further plead, that while no mind, however prolific it may be, can furnish invariably for the pulpit new views of truth and duty, it has been my desire and effort always to present some new light, though it might be in following out a familiar and beaten track. Love of the sanctuary; devotional feeling, to which it is intimately allied, illumined and warmed by ever-brightening rays from the Supreme Intelligence, and joined to a fixed purpose to open the whole soul to their reception and influence, — it has been my main object to excite and cherish. As an habitual attendance on religious services contributes largely to insure their good effects, it may not be out of place here to mention, that public worship has not, during my ministry, been intermitted in this parish for a single sabbath. Our altar-fires have not gone out or slumbered; or, if they have, it has been only that they might be renewed with each returning Sunday.

The ordinances, so simple, so fitting as seals of Christian discipleship and communion, and, furthermore, as means of holiness, it has been a strenuous aim with me, not officially alone, but from strong inclination and conviction, to explain, and urge on your observance; and I rejoice that the appeals of the gospel respecting these have been here complied with by so considerable a number, for themselves and those committed in Providence to their charge. The fifty among us who have, the present season, become stated communicants at the Lord's table, and the seventy who have been baptized into the Holy Spirit, show conclusively, that with us, at least, the ordinances are not dying out. Yet how many even here have not accepted these proffered means of grace! — proffered freely as the gospel itself. How many neglect to offer the children God has given them, at the baptismal font which, through his dear Son, the Saviour of all, who took little children in his arms and blessed them, he has instituted! How many turn from the memorial of Jesus; are deaf to the touching tones of the parting request or precept, or rather both in one, that comes to them from the sublime and beautiful rite before us, — "This do in remembrance of me"! How many have gone to their graves lamenting, when too late, that they had not listened to this, their Saviour's voice! How many, it is to be apprehended, are on their way thither, to have their last moments disturbed by the same painful, unavailing regrets! Is it not time (I submit to you, my friends) for the mass of our religious societies to rouse from this lethargy, — to tear away the veil of mystery and indecision which has so long hung like the pall of death on this interesting and sacred subject? It certainly is full time that the mystical associations which have enveloped it for ages should be swept away, as earth-born fogs, as unnatural and pernicious delusions, from every mind and conscience around which they still hover. The ordinances of Baptism and the Supper, the two and only Christian ordinances, are simply instrumental means to be used by all who have the desire and discretion to employ them for their own or others' benefit; and this congregation, and every one claiming to be Christian, in which they are not so used by all who can realize the solemn duty of observing them, are far below the standard of our religion, — are palpably deficient in one of its chief requirements.

Were they thus observed and employed, the Church would take her rightful position, — would stand where she stood in the early ages, when all believers, with their children, were, through the ordinances, taken to the bosom of her visible family, and before custom and fashion had gathered around her a vast company, who, though coming to her worship, refrain from the observance of her distinguishing rites. She would then be indeed a living church. The congregation would thus be virtually resolved into the church; which to my mind is far wiser and better than — what has with no little ability been advocated — merging the latter in the former. "Ah!" many will exclaim, "then we must subscribe a creed; must enter into a covenant; must make a profession, and profess more than we are prepared to; must, besides, submit to the abridgment of Christian liberty." To such we may reply by asking, What creed is requsite, beyond belief in Jesus as the Christ? which is all the New Testament demands, and to which every Christian might yield a ready assent. Why not covenant for the promotion of religious purposes, when you associate for so many other less important ones? Can profession, or confession,— as we may perhaps better say, though both are scriptural terms,— which is joined to belief of the heart in the means of salvation, and which we make without the trials undergone by confessors and martyrs in other regions and times, —can it be otherwise than productive of strength in ourselves and others for a true consecration to the Christian life? Do the bonds, by which the members of a church are united, imply necessarily any infringement of personal rights or freedom? or do they tend, or can they be perverted, to any which may not be prevented, certainly be remedied, by the ultimate and inalienable right of resignation? These questions, it seems to me, are answered in the asking. So far as the views they suggest have been followed out, they have never, to my knowledge, occasioned complaints of oppression, or regret for having practically complied with them. On the contrary, compliance with them, I have uniformly found, has been felt by the practisers of it to be a high privilege and rich blessing. Fully convinced of their correctness and blessed tendencies, it has been my earnest endeavor to procure their practical adoption among us, to the extent of the nearest possible approximation to identity of church and congregation; and I hope, my friends, that you will not rest, till this object, in itself so desirable and important,— which the simple views we hold so favor, and, if fairly carried out, are sure to effect,— shall be completely secured.

Another institution, worthy to be named in immediate connection with the church, which some are ready — and not without reason — to regard as second only to that, in the useful agencies of the world, is the Sunday school. Whatever the forms in which it has existed, since its establishment by Robert Raikes, of England, in the last century, it has been founded in and sustained by the very spirit of Him among whose last injunctions was, "Feed my lambs." Here, on this spot, was established the first regular parish Sunday school in New England, and perhaps throughout Christendom. First gathered from among the forsaken and destitute, and the debased and vicious, by two noble women of our society, in 1810, it soon was warmly adopted by other members, with the pastor, and became in its essential organization what it has ever since remained. During that time, there has arisen a very large body of teachers and pupils, who have received great mutual benefit, and also been fitted to strengthen and adorn the church and the community. In both portions of this body have been those, not a few, of high intellectual and moral endowments, and of eminence in public and private life. A majority of our present number have shared in its direct benefits. Who of us has not been indirectly benefited by it? Particularly has it, and have we, been favored in its superintendents.

Previously to the worthy incumbent, there have been but three. The first was Robert Rantoul [of whom, now that his venerable form is no more seen among us, I may speak in print, as his personal presence forbade me to do in the delivery of this discourse]. He had the sagacity to discern in the sabbath school, at the outset, a prime element of social and moral progress, and, for many years, freely gave to its supervision his best powers; and never after, to his dying day, ceased to regard it with tender and watchful interest. The charge was relinquished by him to one singularly fitted to sustain and grace it, — William Thorndike, alike respected and dearly beloved among us; all too early lost; withdrawn from us at the scarcely meridian age of forty, though not till he had been distinguished in the legal profession, in various walks of business, and as the dignified and admired presiding head of our State Legislature; and not till he had planted a name and memory, that now, after the lapse of more than a score of years, are fresh as with the morning dew, and fragrant with the odor of sanctity. He continued in the discharge of this important and sacred trust until declining health compelled its resignation. He was succeeded by Albert Thorndike, to whom with him might apply the exclamation, *Par nobile fratrum*, — Two noble brothers; both commanding in person, of elevated bearing, courteous and benevolent in spirit, intelligent, high-minded, pure in principle, aiming — and remarkably successful in their aim — to divide rightly their superior powers between worldly and spiritual pursuits. The latter, we feel but too sensibly, has just gone to take his place by the side of the former in the spirit-world. Lovely and honored in their lives, they are no longer separated by death. That mourning drapery with which our orchestra is clad bespeaks but imperfectly the new grief for him, who, by his decease at the mature yet vigorous age of fifty-eight, when so much more of usefulness was anticipated, has vacated a place which from his youth he had occupied there, and ceased from the active and leading part, which for most of that time he took, not only in the music of the temple, but in tuning the voice, and training the mind and heart, of the young, to the service of their Creator.

Such are the men that have condescended — rather counted it no condescension, but a high privilege and holy

pleasure — to lay aside weighty public and private responsibilities, and devote themselves to Sunday-school instruction. While they were here thus engaged, the names
and characters of Leverett Saltonstall, Stephen C. Phil-
lips, and others of eminent worth, were associated with
similar services in neighboring parishes. These all felt
that the ground they thus occupied was holy ground,
that the time so spent was hallowed time, and that the
vigilance and energies thus exerted were consecrated to
one of the noblest works in which they could be employed.
For myself, I feel that the hours I have uniformly passed in
the school have been among the most delightful and im-
proving in my own experience, and the most satisfying and
fruitful of good in ministering to others.

It may justly be expected of every Christian pastor to
watch and labor especially for the young. No part
of the care devolved on me has been more cheerfully
and assiduously executed than this, whether it was to
be exercised for them in or out of their homes, on the
sabbath or the week day, in the private or public schools;
which last — as from my coming here, one year excepted, I
have been a member of the General Committee, and, most
of that period, its chairman — have claimed and received
a large share of my time and attention. But, for whatever
it may have been in my power so to do for the young, I
have been richly rewarded by their friendship; and yet
more by what I have witnessed of their progress in knowledge, virtue, and preparation for future usefulness, honor,
and happiness. To their continued attachment, and the
fulfilment of their early promise, and the rich satisfac-
tion of seeing them useful, honored, and prosperous in the

world, do I look forward for much of the support and solace of advancing age.

In the discharge of the duties designated peculiarly as pastoral, it has been my aim and pleasure to enter, by a sympathy full, free, divested of mere formality, into the condition and wants of all to whom I stood in the endearing and sacred relation of a pastor to his people. To impart light and encouragement to the inquiring, doubting, or despondent; to sympathize with the sorrowing or rejoicing, comfort the afflicted, provide for the destitute, sustain and cheer the sick and dying; to bury the dead; to do that which actual experience only can tell how trying it is, — leading in the last sad offices to them on whom we reposed as true and dear friends, — this, and whatever else is included in the sphere of pastoral duty, have I desired to perform seasonably, tenderly, faithfully. For all the co-operation and encouragement I have received in this delicate, and often difficult, part of ministerial service, I would make grateful acknowledgment. At the same time, I would suggest that pastoral exertion might, here and generally, be rendered far more effective than it is by a free communication of wants, doubts, difficulties; by letting it be known when and where aid is needed, and may be most effectually applied.

In reviewing the last eight and twenty years, I realize almost with wonder the degree to which my existence has been here concentrated. In this appointed sphere of duty have centred mainly my thoughts, feelings, and interests, during that long period. While I have wished and sought to meet all just claims on my services from abroad, which of necessity have been many and various, I have felt that ministerial faithfulness, like charity, begins at home, and should be principally exhibited there. Here, accordingly, I have chiefly aimed to be useful, and with a steadiness of effort, which, I confess, has at times seemed too continuous. Scarce a day in this large space of time has been without its burden of care and sympathy, such as sometimes to weigh heavily on the spirits, and task severely the energies of both mind and body. If ever there has appeared a want of sensibility in my public or private ministrations, I cheerfully leave it, after due allowance is made for the official need and advantage of self-control, to be set to the account of human imperfection. Of this, not I alone, but most pastors and preachers, could assure you, that often they are constrained to be calm when it would be a relief, indeed, to weep. If my labors have not been strenuous and abundant as some, and myself not least, might wish, I would fain trust that something will be pardoned to the discretion which takes warning from the many deplorable instances — and my own profession has furnished its full share — of those who have attained a premature lustre only to undergo an untimely and disastrous eclipse; and who, by overstrained zeal in the morning of their usefulness, have forfeited their meridian vigor, and unfitted themselves for bearing the burden and heat of the day. If I have not literally fulfilled the injunction preached from at my ordination, — "Give thyself wholly to them," — still no small part of what I was or had have been here bestowed. It is, however, with no feigned humility I acknowledge, that the labors of my ministry are far from having accomplished what I could desire; though I gratefully rejoice in whatever result, good in itself, or corresponding to the nature and design of the Christian ministry, may have attended them. But such as they may have been, for good or for evil, to you or me or others, their account must forthwith close, — be summed up and rendered in, to await the sentence of the final bar.

Increased experience, here let me say, has tended to enlarge and confirm my sense of the solemn responsibility of the ministerial office. Not that I have been led to view that office as alone solemn and clothed with weighty responsibilities, or to regard it in any contracted light. Every occupation in life is serious. All rightful occupations in which men can engage are worthy and important. One of the greatest dangers, indeed, to which the Christian pastor's office is exposed, is that of being considered as standing alone, rather than as intimately associated with all employments and duties, having mutual relations with them all, and helping men to do the work of religion, instead of doing it for them. So to consider it must always have the effect to diminish materially its power and usefulness. It is, notwithstanding, a high and holy and blessed office. This I have felt the more, the more I have contemplated the subjects to which it relates; the inquiries it includes and demands; the communion with God and Christ, with the human soul and all souls, to which it leads; the elevation of character and pursuits; the devotion to the best interests of man and society, to truth, righteousness, and heaven, which it prompts and requires. Also and especially has it risen in my estimation, the more I have entered personally and practically into its duties, its pleasures, and even its trials. And though the young man, on first surveying the vast field of its aims and requisitions, may naturally be appalled by its vastness; and the elder laborer, as he becomes better acquainted with it, and sees it continually enlarging in extent, may be oppressed,

if not absolutely disheartened, by his responsibilities, —
it is nevertheless a glorious field in which to work ;
and I thank God for having been permitted so long,
though so poorly, to labor in it. To have well cultivated
that field ; to have won in it the humblest title to the appellation, " Good and faithful servant," — is, in truth, a
crown of righteousness. No greener or brighter wreath
should I desire to wear on my brow, or have laid on my
grave.

Instances of such fidelity have not been wanting in your
ecclesiastical history. It is somewhat more than two centuries since this parish was virtually established. For
rather more than twenty years from the settlement of this
town, its inhabitants worshipped at the First Church in
Salem, of which this place was then a part. In 1649,
owing to their increase in numbers, and the inconvenience
of worshipping at that distance, particularly as they were
obliged to cross the intervening arm of the sea in boats, they
petitioned for leave to form a separate society. This was
at first refused ; but, the following year, the request, having
been renewed, was so far granted as " to authorize the brethren on Bass-River side to procure the service of an able and
approved teacher, they still retaining their connection with
the church in Salem." With this permission, they employed
several religious teachers, till their regular organization as a
church in September, 1667 ; when John Hale, who had for
three years previously ministered to them, was ordained
their pastor. He so continued to his death in May, 1700 ;
having been with them about thirty-six years, and nearly
thirty-three from his ordination. He was acceptable and
faithful in the discharge of his office, and distinguished for
his independence and public spirit. These last traits were

evinced in his accompanying as chaplain, in opposition
to the wishes of his people, an expedition against Canada.
They were more strikingly displayed in the part he took in
that horrid tragedy, — the witchcraft delusion of 1692.
Having favored the prosecution, and assisted in the exami-
nation, of some of the accused, he was suddenly brought to
a pause by the fact, that his own wife, a person of singular
excellence, was "cried out against." Entirely convinced
of her innocence, he was induced thereby (as he states)
to scan more strictly the principles he had imbibed on
this subject, and by scanning to question, and by ques-
tioning at length to reject, many of them. He at once —
and, under the circumstances, it demanded no little moral
courage to do it — set his face against the prevailing current
of superstition. Soon afterward, he prepared and published
a treatise on witchcraft, which the revered John Higginson
commends as a work which the writer's "pious and modest
manner," and his "singular prudence and sagacity in
searching into the narrows of things," would render
"generally acceptable to all the lovers of truth and peace."
A copy of it is preserved with our church-records. It
had undoubtedly a valuable influence in overcoming a delusion which was one of the darkest clouds that ever came
over New England, and that settled with deepest gloom on
this vicinity; during which, it has been truly said, none
could lie down on their pillow, or walk forth in the light of
day, without the most terrible apprehension of being accused, brought to trial, and, without reason, imprisoned, or
dragged away to a cruel and infamous death; and which
was not checked till many had thus suffered, and not a few
had confessed themselves guilty to save their lives.

When their first pastor — who in such varied and trying

scenes, as in the usual sphere of his duty, had served them so well — was called, at the ripe age of sixty-three, from his earthly labors, a grateful people followed him to his rest with tears and fond regrets, with the inscription on their hearts no less than on his gravestone, — "A pious and faithful minister of the gospel;" while his descendants, in successive generations, arose to bear up his honored name, and carry forward the work which he had so nobly commenced.

In October, 1701, his place was supplied by Thomas Blowers; who is described by a cotemporary as a "very valuable man, good scholar, and excellent minister; a distinguished example of warm devotion, of extensive goodness, meekness, and sweetness of temper; of great stability in his principles, and steadiness in his conduct; a very faithful friend and obliging neighbor; a most tender and kind husband and father; a vigilant, prudent pastor, and close, pathetic preacher; had in great veneration among the associated pastors in the vicinity; highly esteemed by all his acquaintance, and universally beloved by his flock." His sudden decease, in the fifty-second year of his age and twenty-eighth of his ministry, was regarded as a severe bereavement by them, and by the whole community, that appreciated his worth, and of which he was a pillar and ornament. Samson Salter Blowers, Chief Justice of the Supreme Court of Nova Scotia, was his grandson; who died in 1842, having attained the age of a hundred years, and been a long time the senior survivor among the graduates of Harvard College; for which the grandfather, more than a century before, had done good service, and shown a filial and enlarged spirit, by publicly meeting the objections against the election of Leverett to its first office, particularly that of his being a layman, and by contributing his aid to secure for it his brilliant presidency.

Joseph Champney, the third pastor, was ordained here in December, 1729, — less than six months after his predecessor's death. His ministry is the longest, by far, yet sustained in this place; having extended into its forty-fourth year, in which he died, at the age of sixty-eight. Without conspicuous ability, he was esteemed and loved for his sincerity, his mild, benevolent, and social disposition, and his devotedness to the good of his parishioners and to the duties of his profession. His life is represented by those who knew him to have been that of a true Christian, and its close was serene and happy. Owing to his impaired health, in 1772, the assistance of a colleague was required; and Joseph Willard was ordained in November of that year. Within three months after his settlement, he, by the death of his senior associate, became sole pastor; and so remained for a little over nine years, till his resignation on being elected President of Harvard University. In that high station he passed the remainder of his life, — nearly twenty-three years; a longer term than, with a single exception, was had by any who have filled it; and deceased in the sixty-sixth year of his age. Though his ministry was comparatively brief, it sufficed to leave here a deep and permanent impression. Rational and liberal in his theology; plain, earnest, practical; aiming at spiritual improvement, rather than display of critical learning, in his public ministrations; in his more private ones wise, kind, sympathizing; respected and influential in the community, through his talents, acquirements, and weight of character, — it was but natural that he should be highly prized by his parish, and parted from with keen regret. "It is with the greatest reluctance," they say in answer to his request for dismissal, "that we think of consenting to our pastor's leaving us, with whom we have lived happily for so long a season. We, though with pain, give him up for the sake of the public; and ardently wish, that, when invested with the president's office, he may be a rich blessing to the world." His character, in the wider sphere to which he was transferred, is too generally and well known to require labored eulogy. Dignified, firm, resolute, judicious, yet condescending and gentle; exercising a truly parental authority; enjoying a reputation for ripe scholarship in classical, and also in mathematical and astronomical, learning; and directing his powers and acquisitions, with great singleness of purpose, to the advancement of the institution over which he presided, — he at once maintained and adorned his eminent position. It has been justly said of him, by one who was both his pupil and associate in government and instruction, that " his unbending integrity, his patience and fidelity in duty, his claims to professional and literary respect and confidence, gave him a high rank among the worthies, guardians, and guides of his generation."

After an interval of about three years, he was succeeded by Joseph McKean, who was settled in May, 1785. He was pastor of this society for seventeen years; during which his reputation, as a sound theologian and solid scholar, was fully established. Of noble and commanding person; with manners and character marked by mingled simplicity and dignity; possessing an intellect clear, strong, sagacious, and discriminating; frank, amiable, generous, Christian, in spirit; as a preacher, felicitously combining instruction and impressiveness; impartial and assiduous in fulfilling his parochial relations, — he was greatly endeared to his people, and highly regarded at large. In 1802, with the very

5

reluctant consent of those with whom he had here been so happily connected, he accepted an invitation to become the first President of Bowdoin College. On the new and important field thus opened to him he entered with profound interest, and gave to it his full energy. But after five years of laborious and faithful service, in the midst of his days and usefulness, when the seed he had so diligently sown was beginning to spring up and bear fruit, he was, in the fiftieth year of his age, summoned from earth; to human view, prematurely and sadly departing; yet not till he had laid an adequate foundation for the distinction and prosperity which the institution, commenced under his fostering care, has since attained.

His successor in the pastorate was Abiel Abbot, who is still freshly remembered among us. Having had a previous settlement of eight years at Haverhill, he came here in 1803, where he passed the remainder of his life; with which his ministry terminated, in its twenty-fifth year, and the fifty-eighth of his age. By inclination and early training, he was formed for the church, and the sacred profession by which peculiarly it is upheld and administered. Inquiring diligently into the truths of Christianity, he abandoned the Trinity, with other kindred doctrines he had originally adopted, and became thoroughly grounded in the Unitarian faith. But, averse to controversy, dreading the evils often accompanying it, and impressed with the superior efficacy of practical religion, he dwelt little on disputed topics, and seldom discussed them in the pulpit. Remarkable for ease, grace, suavity of bearing and address; for ready and fluent utterance; for solemnity, unction, pathos, in delivery; quick, warm, broad, in his sympathies; instructive and entertaining, genial and captivating, in the social circle; with no common resources and powers for informing, moving, swaying a promiscuous assembly, — he was eminently fitted for discharging the functions, retired or public, of his professional calling. Delighting in his office, he magnified it by the sincerest devotion to its duties. His published writings manifest literary culture, much skill in composition, accurate and acute observation of men and things. He had tact to seize, and the vigor as well as the disposition to follow up and improve, opportunities of usefulness, however offered. Of singular aptitude for reaching and attracting the young, and leading them to the pursuit of knowledge and virtue, he left on multitudes of them impressions, in their nature invaluable, and lasting as the minds thus influenced. Our common schools were re-organized under his supervision, and received an impulse and direction from his wise and guiding hand, from which vast benefits will not soon cease to accrue. All the means of intellectual and moral training among us were stimulated by his zeal, and pervaded by the force and beauty of his spirit. Measures for social, moral, and religious reform and elevation, found in him a ready and strong ally; and the numerous benevolent associations, which in his time were springing into existence, had his cordial welcome and aid. The withdrawal of one thus gifted, and an instrument of so much good, could not fail to produce a profound and wide sensation, and a most sad and painful void. Many of you remember the gloom which overspread this entire region when the mournful announcement came, that on his return from a Southern clime, whither he had gone in pursuit of health, he had, while approaching the shore, and a speedy return to his home was fondly anticipated, been arrested by death; and that you should see his face, hear his voice, and be blessed by his presence, no more. Though the lamp of his mortal life has long since gone out, yet the light of his beneficent ministry will shine on, even as they who have turned many to righteousness, perpetual as the stars.

The ministries we have cursorily reviewed, taken with that now closing, average considerably more than a quarter of a century each in duration. It is likewise a noticeable fact, — one honorable alike to them and those they served, — that, excepting the two whose services were claimed for the heads of two of our principal literary institutions, and who, as we have seen, parted from their people with great mutual regard and regrets, all the former pastors of this society died and were lamented as such; death alone dissolving the pastoral tie which bound them in uninterrupted harmony to you, or to them who have preceded you. A circumstance yet more important than either of those just stated is, that while they were all highly respectable for ability, and possessed an amount of talent and acquirement which procured them high honor and influence among cotemporaries and with after-generations, — and in which, as belonging to its succession of pastors, any parish might take a laudable pride, — no stain is recorded, or is related by tradition, to have rested on their characters as men, as Christians, or as ministers of religion. Truly and most significantly may we in this view say, "Sweet is the savor of their names;" precious, indeed, the legacy left in the memory of their purity and worth to those who have or shall come after them; invaluable the moral weight which their example has borne and must ever carry with it, inspiring genuine respect for religion, and winning many to virtue. The impressions thus produced of the dignity, sacredness, and value of the pastoral office, cannot be effaced, or lose their benign efficacy, in this parish and this community. Let me add an expression of the humble hope, glowing ardently in my breast, that if my memory may not be radiant and a fount of good like theirs, and be not your pride, it still may not bring reproach on that sacred office, and not be for your and your descendants' regret and shame.

Though led, by the train we have pursued, to speak more at length of the pastors, I would not, by any means, omit due recognition of the character of them to whom they ministered. That has been marked by general intelligence, benevolence, integrity, and virtue ; by reverence for Religion and her institutions, and observance of them to at least the usual extent. An uncommon proportion of men of eminence has been included in this society; and — what we may re-mark as a particular advantage and blessing — the most influential members have been its firm supporters, and real friends of religion. Two of these stand out in its history with special prominence, — one having been most extensive-ly engaged in its concerns during a large part of the last century; the other, for nearly all which has elapsed of the present one, having had a leading agency in its affairs. The former was Robert Hale, grandson of the first pastor : he was born in 1702, and died in 1767. He was endowed with superior natural abilities, liberally educated, and bred to the medical profession, in which he soon had extensive practice. Intrusted also with important financial interests ; a colonel in the expedition against Louisburg, and dis-tinguished in its capture ; largely occupied in public business of the town, county, and state ; commissioner on repeated and pressing emergencies from our own to other Commonwealths, — he acquitted himself throughout with signal fidelity and ability. Extensive and engrossing as were his other occupations, he yet found time to attend, with characteristic thoroughness, to every thing concerning his native parish, from grave questions of theology and ecclesiastical government, down to — what, to be sure, in his time, was a matter of no slight moment, though we might attach little to it — the framing of a precise code of rules for " seating the meeting-house ; " by which there was a range of many degrees, from the " foremost magistrate seat " to those assigned to the unmarried and to persons greatly in debt among the humblest. — The other name, which, from its connection with the parish, may be appropriately coupled with his, is Robert Rantoul. To him I have already alluded, for the part he took in the Sunday school. It was not there alone that he manifested lively and active interest for the young, but in all the institutions and means by which they might be benefited. That interest, early begun and sustained, personally and officially, through many years, abated not with advanced age. It was touching to see him, his head white with the snows of more than seventy winters, moving amid youthful assemblies, whether gathered for instruction or amusement, and observe his sterner aspect relax and soften as he entered by cordial sympathy into their pursuits and pleasures. For the reformatory and philanthropic enterprises of the day, he was also strongly interested ; and in some of them, especially that of promoting temperance, he was among the pioneers, and, in certain respects, took the initiative. He was, for upwards of twenty years, a representative or a senator in the General Court, where, from talent and experience, he had an influence rarely exerted by a single individual ; was on several commissions from the State ; and was a member of the convention for revising its Constitution in 1820, and again in that of 1853; in the last of which he was recognized as its Nestor, and called to preside at its organization. The services which, in spheres less extensive and nearer home, he rendered, were very numerous, various, and valuable. Noted as he was for the punctilious and persevering discharge of all his duties, there is no respect in which, with this parish and church, he is more entitled to high consideration and grateful remembrance, than the uniform devotedness with which, as officer and member, for more than half a century, he took a leading part in their proceedings, and studied their interests. His honorable and useful life was prolonged to within a month of the completion of his eightieth year, and terminated in a peaceful departure.

Among the patriarchs of the society, on my coming to it, were Nathan Dane and Joshua Fisher. As I saw those two venerable men at the head of the procession leading to my ordination, I could not but view the circumstance as presenting a marked feature in the then existing condition of the parish, and an auspicious omen for the future. The former was a lawyer by profession (one which has been remarkably represented, by numbers, ability, and character, in our congregation); the father, as he has been called by high authority, of American law; author of the immortal ordinance for the government of the North-western Territory, by which slavery was for ever excluded from that immense and now populous region; withal, of unimpeachable integrity and purity. His mind was richly stored with theological knowledge. He devoted much time — giving his sabbaths exclusively — to its acquisition; was a constant attendant on public worship, even after deafness

had disabled him from listening to it ; and a liberal con-
tributor to its support. The latter — a learned and skil-
ful physician ; President of the Massachusetts Medical Society ; a proficient in natural science ; a senator of the Com-
monwealth, and deeply interested in civil affairs ; an able and
faithful officer in institutions of business and charity ; in all
the relations of life upright, high-minded, and worthy — is
to be esteemed, in the distribution of his wealth, though
far more in his life and example, a great public benefactor
to this his adopted parish ; pecuniarily, the largest. While
his bounty flowed freely in various other channels, the
ample fund, which, with the aid of Israel Thorndike, — himself a generous friend and son of the parish, — he established
for the support of the ministry in it, will cause him to be
ever gratefully remembered among us. I may add, that
from the three last named, and Moses Brown, — also an honored parishioner, — donations and legacies to the amount of
fifty thousand dollars have gone to Harvard University, for
which strong interest has always here existed ; where all the
ministers of this society, one only excepted, were graduated ;
and over which, we have seen, one of them long and wor-
thily presided.

An enlightened liberality in sentiment, feeling, action, is
seen sending the current of its warm and healthy life-blood
through our whole parochial existence. That which seeks
out and promotes good objects, whether within or without its immediate circle, and, because manifest in deeds,
is least to be suspected, has, I trust, been in good degree —
if not to the extent justly desirable — exercised. The diffusion of intelligence by personal effort, by books, libraries,
schools, and higher seminaries, or by any other methods
deemed expedient, has been a favorite object, and has received,

from those qualified to further it, strong countenance and
aid. That there is more of truth to break forth continually
from God's word and works; that the firmament of knowledge, common and sacred, is absolutely boundless, and
should be constantly explored; which was uttered in substance, and partly in these very terms, by the Pilgrim Father,
Robinson,—has been steadily maintained. Perfect freedom
of investigation into both nature and revelation is a standing declaration of our creed; or would be, if we had any
other one than that of the Bible. The records of this
church show that the terms of communion have never been
narrow or exclusive, and that censures have never been
inflicted for supposed error of opinion. Its independence
has been firmly upheld. The proposal of a convention of
ministers at Boston, in 1705, for consociating the Con-
gregational churches, found little if any more favor here
than did a similar one from the Massachusetts General
Association in 1814, which, like the former, encountered an
opposition so strenuous as to lead to its abandonment. The
Cambridge Platform of ecclesiastical government was not
formally adopted by this church till nearly seventy years
after its organization; and then only with essential modifi-
cations and reservations, among which was this,— that the
Platform should be received in " their own sense," or as
the members chose to understand and apply it. These, and
many other facts and considerations that might be adduced,
sufficiently indicate the independent tone which has prevailed in maintaining the rights of the church as a body,
and of the individuals composing it.

The relations, however, of this society, both within and
without itself, have, from the beginning to the present time,
been singularly peaceful and harmonious. Few councils, al-

most none (none, surely, since my connection with it), have been summoned for advice or arbitration in the settlement of disputes and difficulties. No differences of sentiment or action have arisen, that have resulted in permanent controversy, alienation, or division, and that have not been quickly followed by reconciliation, or agreement to differ, or, at most, quiet withdrawal. Unity of the spirit in the bond of peace has been the motto of practice, for yourselves and your predecessors, in relation to those within your borders and to other religious societies. Between the mother church — the first in Salem — and this, and between the ministers and people of both, there has always been the most friendly union. For seventeen years after they had separate worship, they met — in beautiful token of Christian fellowship and love — at the same table of communion. They have kept pace together in what we consider the advance of religious ideas. They bear, as they have long borne, the same distinctive appellation among the denominations of Christians. May their only strife henceforth be, as it has hitherto been, striving together for the faith of the gospel. So has it been, so may it ever be, in the relation of this to the first-born of the churches that have sprung from it, with which we have always been in peculiar connection and sympathy; and she to-day has affectingly recognized these, by suspending her usual service, and joining with us on this parting occasion. For her, and for all the congregations of the town, whether of like or differing faith, do we wish, from the fruitful and loving parent of them all, at this hour, and out of the house of God, prosperity, and his peace to keep them for ever in perfect peace.

A character for stability, moreover, may justly be attributed to this parish. Here, where, for two centuries and more, divine worship and the ordinances of religion have been statedly observed, where a succession of ministers — with less than usual interruption — has been sustained, and where, through all that extended period, wise and good and devout men have watched and prayed, endured and persevered, we may look for something stable, and not, I trust, look in vain. Not the stability which dwells in the past, rests where they who preceded us stood, abjures innovation, denies the claim of any superiority of light or virtue in the present over the ages gone; still less that which contents itself with inactivity, and neither cherishes the desire, nor puts forth effort, for a higher and better spiritual life than has yet been reached: but that which looks before and around no less than behind; with due veneration for the past, mingles just reference to the present and the future; moves forward with open eye and elastic step, ready to discern and walk in the ways, commands, and ordinances, and through the scenes of duty and trial, designed by Heaven, and to which its unerring finger points. An enlightened conservatism, combined with earnest desire and endeavor after progress, and based on the scriptural formula, — steadfast and immovable, always abounding in the work of the Lord, — has with us been sought, and, we will hope, in some good measure, though very far from what it should have been, attained. This is the only stability on which, as individuals, as members of society, or a Christian church, we can, amid the vicissitudes of earth, and under the grand law of change passed on all human things, securely repose.

How wide and unceasing is the operation of that law! What change has been going on since this spot was set apart and consecrated to religious uses, to which it has from the first been devoted, for the place of our worship!

During that period, our country has been mostly reclaimed from the savage and from solitude, and our nation all but created. Who can describe, or merely count, the changes that have in that period taken place relating to material, social, and religious objects, the world of matter and mind within and around us? The spot itself — while so many and varying lights and shadows have been passing over it — how changed, from the lowly temple that stood near the site of our vestry, the humble nature of which is indicated by a vote passed sixteen years after its erection, " that the meeting-house be ceiled up to the wall-plates, rabbeted, and the windows glazed," — through the second, erected in 1682, which was superior to the first, but was rude in its style and construction, as we may infer from its having been without " laths and plaster," open to the " ridge-pole," and its floor having not, till forty years after it was built, been laid " on the beams with boards and joist," — down to the third house, erected in 1770, enlarged in '95, remodelled and for the most part rebuilt in 1835; since which its interior has been improved and beautified, and rendered commodious and pleasant as we now see it! If the place and temples show change, much more do the worshippers. With the eye of fancy, and in the light of authentic record, we look, as on a movable panorama, upon the assemblies from age to age here gathered. We see the earlier ones ranged in order and lines, according to rank, age, sex, condition, or other qualifications, prescribed by rule, except where particular positions were assigned by way of reward or favor; and the later ones, with some variations, arranged after the methods customary in our own time. In each we see reflected its peculiar manners, habits, culture; its appointed discipline of good and evil, joy and sorrow, temptation and trial. As we see these all, so varying and transitory as they have been, we enter more fully than we before have done into the changing nature of human life and experience, and realize how changeful as well as rapid is the stream on which the generations of men, and ourselves among them, are borne onward.

Instead, however, of further looking through the two centuries that have passed over this parish, it is enough only to glance at the variegated aspect of the events which have occurred since we have been together during my pastorate. In that comparatively brief period, how have society and the world altered! and what a new face has come on both! Wonderful discoveries and inventions have been multiplied, by which the domain of science has been vastly extended, man's social condition essentially varied and improved, and the material creation itself greatly changed. Mighty revolutions have shaken nations to their foundation, and thrones have been set up and overturned. Peace and war have had their alternations in our own and most other countries. New theories in government, morals, and religion, have been broached; have had their day, and been exploded. New truths have been proclaimed, and brought into use; old ones have been set in new and better lights, and so rendered more beneficial. And though an awful cloud of sin casts its shadow, like a foul blot, on the earth, and on all the souls living upon it, and vice and crime stalk abroad in high places and low, I still believe that the world, for the last quarter-century, has not stood still or receded, but has, on the whole, and in vital respects, been gaining.

What changes, too, have time and death — not to name other causes — wrought around and in the midst of us in the period we are contemplating! Those who, at the commencement of it, were the venerated elders and pillars in church and state, — the fathers, — where are they? You will, perhaps, be surprised at the fact, that none of the pastors of the fourteen societies of our denomination in Essex County remain where, at the beginning of my ministry, I found them; and only three of them are among the living. The patriarchs of the council convened at the time of my ordination — all the aged persons, also, then belonging to the parish — have since passed away. The then middle-aged have grown old; the then young have glided into maturity. Nearly an entire generation has come upon the stage of life, while another has left it. A congregation of itself has been added from among us to the congregation of the dead. — Here we pause to drop the tear of remembrance for the many whom Death has not permitted to continue with us; whom that stern reaper has gathered in, whether in the early flower, or mature vigor, or full ripeness. At the call of memory, there is scarcely a seat here, or house, or family; "no flock, however tended;" scarcely a region of earth or a sea, — that does not give up our dead. In all kindness and tenderness, we greet their images as they rise freshly to view. For some, officers and members, tried friends and supporters, of this church and society, and of whatever is good, the tears of recent and sad bereavement freely flow. Do we not still hear the sound of departing wings as their spirits take the upward flight? Do they not seem to linger, that they may dispense heavenly benedictions, and give parting assurances that their guardian care and love will not cease to watch over these scenes they loved so well?

Great and often trying as are the changes and the whole

vicissitude of life, we can hardly doubt their necessity, any more than we can escape their occurrence. Because they have no changes, says a sacred oracle, they fear not God. These are needed by men and Christians, alone and individually, or in groups and societies. They are often indispensably necessary to arrest attention, and prompt to vigilance and exertion. A quiet, undisturbed current of events has done unspeakable harm to men, and to bodies of men, by lulling to indifference, negligence, and inefficiency; and so banishing, not only the fear of God, but concern and zeal for the welfare of man. Even harmony and peace may thus become the bane of a Christian society and church. Welcome, then, change. Let it come; let it come fast and often, and in all its Heaven-appointed variety. It is a blessed monitor and guide; it may be, a comforter and healer. It brings balm from Gilead, — a medicine for the mind, from the great Physician. By it souls may be reformed, enlarged, built up to celestial grace and beauty; to sum all in two words, — sanctified, saved. And though it may at times be trying, and hard to bear; may administer a rude shock; be appalling even to the sensibilities; may be for the present not joyous, but grievous; and we might not be prepared to delight in it for its own sake, — we may yet rejoice in the blessing it carries with it, of which we are invited, nay urged, to partake in full. We may, moreover, rejoice that the changing universe is presided over and ordered by Him who doeth all things rightly and well; who has and needs no changes; with whom is no variableness, or shadow of turning; and in whom we may repose unchanging and perfect trust.

Notwithstanding the numerous and varied scenes through which we have passed together since we were joined in the

sacred ties that unite pastor and people, it is difficult for
me to realize how extended the space of time thus traversed.
So under bright and propitious skies, through green pastures,
and by still waters, has our course been; so harmonious have
been our relations, and mutual and joint action; and, in looking back on them, — having no note of discord, no asperities
of feeling, not an unkind word or look, that I am aware of,
to disturb or mar the review, but bathed, as it were, in an
atmosphere of love and good-will, — I feel like a traveller
beguiled as to the length of his way by its pleasantness.
In the first sermon after my ordination, I said, " Here would
I live and work; and here, in your service, would I have
my earthly labors and conflicts end."   I then thought, if it
should be God's will, and for our reciprocal benefit, to live and
die, their chosen and devoted pastor, among this my own
people.   Being, however, not of firm constitution, I expected my ministry, if continued to the close of my life,
long ere this to have terminated, and to have passed, with
my soul, before the final Judge.   But it has been otherwise
appointed.

And now it only remains for me to bid you, my respected
and beloved parishioners, adieu; which I utter, not so much
as indicative of parting, much less of final leave, as in
its higher meaning, — God be with you.   So I say, Farewell:
in the most literal sense, fare ye well!   May you partake
most richly of temporal and spiritual good!   My earnest
hope is, that, present or absent, I may hear of your affairs,
that ye stand fast in the unity, order, purity, and excellence
of our holy faith, and are constantly strengthened and
elevated therein.   Especially is it my desire that you may
be endued with the highest wisdom for the choice of one to
fill the place now to be vacated.   If, in due season, a pastor

after your own hearts, and approved of God, be granted you, my heart, I assure you, will equally rejoice, and one of its dearest wishes be fulfilled. Be assured, also, that the kindness here shared by me and mine, and the sweet counsel and many happy days and years we have had together, will not fade from my memory; that the tenderest chords of my breast will not cease to vibrate in unison with your welfare; and that my fervent prayers will continually ascend for Heaven's best blessings on you and yours, with whom I have been so long, so intimately, and so sacredly associated.

# APPENDIX.

THE following is a copy of Mr. THAYER'S letter of resignation, and of the record of proceedings of the parish in answer to it: —

BEVERLY, April 6, 1858.

Hon. ROBERT RANTOUL.

DEAR SIR, — I resign into your hands, and through you, as Chairman of the Standing Committee, to the First Parish, the pastoral office, which, for considerably more than a quarter of a century, has been so harmoniously, and to myself so happily, sustained. My resignation, I propose, should take effect on the 1st of July next. This step has not been taken without earnest deliberation, and a deep sense of the tender and sacred ties which bind, and always will bind, me to the people to whom I have ministered during so                lapse of time, with the changing aspects of th                well suggest not wholly justify, it; b least, from the labors of other claims and duties. my present relation to the trust, that its prosperity will and with the assurance of welfare of all its members

Most res

A communication from the Rev. CHRISTOPHER T. THAYER, in which he proposes to resign his pastoral relations to this parish, having been read and considered, it was thereupon unanimously voted to accept thereof.

*Resolved*, That we deeply regret the impaired condition of his health, which (with other considerations of a private nature) has rendered it necessary for him to ask a release from pastoral labors ; and, in view of the dissolution of a connection now of more than twenty-eight years' standing, we rejoice that it has been so harmoniously and happily sustained during the whole of this period, and that the separation takes place with only the kindest feelings on the part of pastor and people.

Penetrated with the strong expressions of the affectionate interest of our pastor in every member of his parish, in accepting his resignation, we would cordially reciprocate the kind sentiments he has expressed towards us, and offer him our best wishes for the restoration of his health, and a continuance of his usefulness and happiness.

*Resolved*, That his faithful and arduous labors through the whole duration of his ministry, in relation to the municipal interests of the town, deserve the grateful recollection and acknowledgment of the people; and we earnestly hope that a continued residence among us will enable us to enjoy, as heretofore, the influence of his example, the benefit of his talents and varied experience, and of his labo                           ocial, moral, and reli-
us condition

                                                        copy of resolutions passed
                                                        bers of the First Parish in


                                ROBERT RANTOUL,
                                        *Parish Clerk.*